Hello Tommy Trojan!

Aimee Aryal

Illustrated by Gerry Perez

MASCOT BOOKS

www.mascotbooks.com

It was a beautiful fall day at the
University of Southern California.

Tommy Trojan was riding
his horse, Traveler, to the Coliseum
to watch a football game.

He passed by Doheny Library.

Some students walking by yelled,
"Hello Tommy Trojan!"

Tommy Trojan rode through Alumni Park.
He went over to the statue of
Tommy Trojan.

He waved, "Hello Tommy Trojan!"

Tommy Trojan stopped in front
of Bovard Auditorium.

A professor passing by said,
"Hello Tommy Trojan!"

Tommy Trojan went by Heritage Hall.

A group of USC fans standing outside
signaled "V" for Victory and shouted,
"Hello Tommy Trojan!"

It was almost time for the football game.
Tommy Trojan rode to the Coliseum
and met some alumni standing nearby.

The alumni remembered Tommy Trojan
from when they went to USC.
They said, "Hello, again, Tommy Trojan!"

Finally, Tommy Trojan arrived
at the Coliseum.

As he rode Traveler onto the football field, the crowd cheered, "Let's Go Trojans!"

Tommy Trojan watched the game
from the sidelines and
cheered for the team.

The Trojans scored six points!
The quarterback shouted,
"Touchdown Tommy Trojan!"

At half-time the Spirit of Troy band
performed on the field.

Tommy Trojan and the crowd sang,
"Fight On!"

The USC Trojans won
the football game!

Tommy Trojan gave Coach Carroll
a high-five. The coach said,
"Great game Tommy Trojan!"

After the football game, Tommy Trojan was tired. It had been a long day at the University of Southern California.

He walked home and climbed into bed.

"Goodnight Tommy Trojan."

For Anna and Maya and all of
Tommy Trojan's little fans. ~ AA

For my brother Marc, who showed me how far
my imagination can take me. ~ GP

Special thanks to:

Sharon Adamson

Pete Carroll

Margaret Farnum

Frank Gelbart

Elizabeth Kennedy

For information please contact Mascot Books,
P.O. Box 220157, Chantilly, VA 20153-0157.

TOMMY TROJAN, TROJANS, USC, UNIVERSITY OF SOUTHERN CALIFORNIA
are registered trademarks of the University of Southern California and are used under license.

COLISEUM and LOS ANGELES MEMORIAL COLISEUM are registered trademarks of the
Los Angeles Memorial Coliseum Commission and are used under license.

ISBN: 1-932888-08-X

Printed in the United States

www.mascotbooks.com